THE ECHO OF INTIMACY

THE WORSHIP OF TEARS

SUMEET KUMAR

ISBN 979-888546285-3

Sumeet Kumar

Sumeet Kumar , A adult who experiences many phases of love in his life , get broked many times , stands up every time and keep moving to the next phases of the life.In reality he is a writter as well as singer (as a hobby).

Very exciting and interesting fact about him is that he is aauthor of New era i.e. he starts his journey of writing at the age when he was going to schools to get the study.His some famous works i.e. Maturity Of Love (Genre - Love),Privacy For Dream (Genre - Middle Class), Army Squad ofLove (Genre- The Seperation of Army Love), 5 Days of Love(Genre- Temporarily Love), Th e Endearment Of Love(Genre - Historical Era Of Love), Social Destruction Indo-Pak (Genre - The Story of The Love At The Time Of Division Of India And Pakistan), Middle Class Soul (Genre - The Dreams of Middle Class), The Accursed Kanatpur (Genre -The Horrific Story Of A Village), Wrong Number (Genre -The Suspenseful Physco Killer Story), The Secrecy OfDeadly Midnight (Genre - The Suspense About a Crime),Fragile Religious Of Death (Genre- The Death Of A TrustfulPerson), Nature Vs Science (Genre - The Future Battle Between Nature And Science In A Horrific Way), Generic Man (Genre - The Dream of I.I.T), The Unconsious 12 Hours(Genre - The Illusion At Stage Of Comma), The StrangeBurden (Genre - The Burden Of Love) , Her Existence (Genre- The Female Pain In The Society) , Jockstrap Prize (Genre -The True Story Of A National Athlete) , H Man [Hindi] (Genre - Superhero Tragic Story), H Man [English] (Genre - Superhero Tragic Story) , Maturity Of Love [Englsih] (Genre - Love). are available on various geners on the offcial platform of **Amazon, Flipkart and Notionpress**. You can buy them from there.

Contents

PREFACE

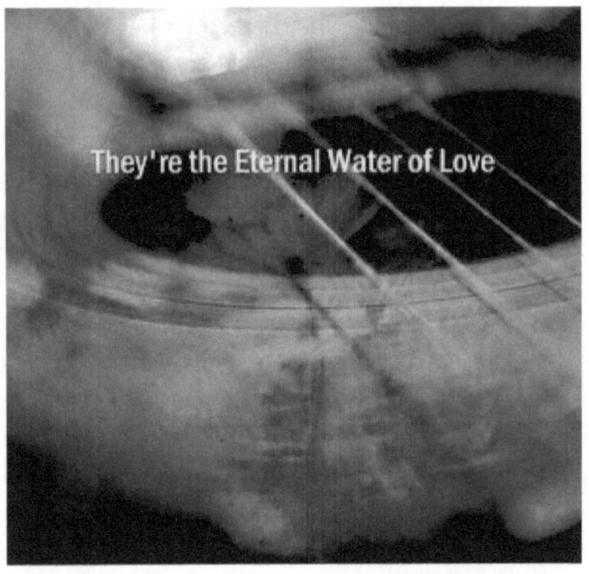

I don't know my identity nor anyone told me, but still, if you listen to this, then maybe you will be relieved to hear how many side effects of one sided relationship are there. If identity was made, then Ambani would keep this Tata Birla in today's time because he never runs after emotions because he believes that the biggest trouble starts with him and ends with him. I don't deserve feet I don't think I'm not worth because a family is what it's a friend This someone's love who doesn't give you your place even after you're gone

Did it. Somebody said that you are mmature, then someone said that nothing can happen to you in life and someone said this but our friendship is not worthy.

Knowing the reason, I have been accused of this. He has made us, he sends us a change from the very beginning. The story is not a big one, because emotions were so big that the story was not long (there was no film with love, I had a short perfect love story like everyone else. Wouldn't have heard of so many villains and heroes, what should I do, this is a film. Not that I should add any other additional character and neither am I the co-director who should change the script because he is watching us sitting above heaven from the arm... don't know the identity of himself and don't tell me feet still if you do this hearing then maybe you will get it after hearing that one sided relationship has kitneside effects..Way it's me sanat (my name means lord brahma by foot name if ambani keeps this tata birla in today's time in identity made because he never got emotions Do not run after because they believe that the biggest trouble begins with them and ends with them) Everyone in my life has left me, By saying that you are not worthy of anyone, I do not think that I am not worthy because a family only This is a friend, it is someone's love that will give you someone else even after you are gone don't give me your place Our friendship is not worthy.. My one question is to all those who have accused me of this without knowing the reason. Who are these people and why should I believe that if we change today at the behest of someone, then we have made that initiative. From now on we send our money back. The story is not a big one, because emotions were so big that the story was not long (there was no film with love, I had a short perfect love story like everyone else. Wouldn't have heard of so many villains and heroes, what should I do, this is a film. Not that I should add any other additional character and neither am I the co-director who should change the script because he is watching us sitting on the arm above heaven

...

Acknowledgements

AMAN KUMAR

Special Thanks to **Aman Kumar** who worked so hard
in the preparation of this book. He has continually put
with my passive voice, omission of words, and late night
calls. You have be en wonderful. Thanks to him for his
precious time in reviewing proposals , individual chapters
and early drafts, along with his suggestions on the
applicability of the material to the world.

I

The Dead Meeting

My life would be so bad in Teenager, I never thought in my childhood that I used to have a wish that when I will grow up, this wishful day ended completely, the day I met all the three villains of my life, however, every film has a story that whatever happens. After all, only the hero wins, it is in the last. Feet want to win in my life I didn't even know that ,You are the hero of life Realizing that the things in life that are never said to be done, it would have given a triple love action. That too in a moment and what is not expected to happen, it also happens after all... It is because we have forgotten that this life is a whole circle (the earthshape is also circle) I will say one thing for sure that if the front end is one, then it is never lost and win, after all, the people considers it better ...as whenever we have exams, it remains quite a box to achieve the rank which is destined for an intelligent person. In a happy way, our life is exactly the same and it is also the same. I feel scared even thinking ahead. They are able to believe where nothing is to be seen other than the four walls, they live in such a captivity where nothing is seen except to remain deserted. In the quest to do, we are giving our soul to someone else. The happiness seen in the eyes would have been saved if no one had given reason for the silence in the eyes, the time would have been saved if someone had found my wrist and did this Would have said that bash was a lot of pain, now let's go back. In the story of the teacher, I will not stay with you, I do not say in your story that you listen to the story of a single such lovers, whose wish was also incomplete and his story too. So don't wait now because there is no time.... let's start it ..

"

"I have erased my existence in the success of his

Love,
but the pond has been left to talk that I am still
alive in his thoughts.
It is a different matter of one sided love that
the witness with
which we are infatuated with someone else's
love..."

II
The Losses Of Time

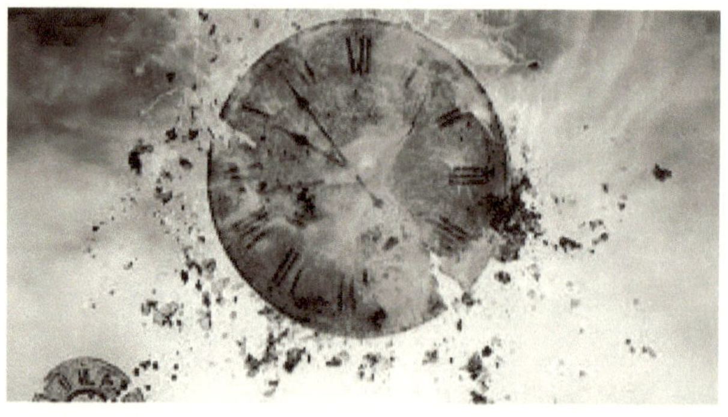

Everything was fine in my life, before her arrival, I used to say a lot to do and like the rest, I had many big dreams, by the way, let me tell one thing about myself that I am a neat aspirants student and I am very fond of singing songs in my free time. What I knew was that the person who writes in writing for someone and for his sake, maybe undefined memories is like a poison if he entered the body, neither did his excitement, if we did not come out, then go ahead The face of death is also a hypocrisy.. I am feeling a little vaquard because you have never told anyone about it, but it is important that today I should talk about everything, because of which any one person goes to society for work, it is enough for me .in the way of losses of time we already said that (stability of love is dependent on different age which they live in government) in my life also my age matters a lot because the society of the age of love I am still in the imagination would have happened before meeting with her , the society would have known that love is nothing. It is an illusion of emotions, the closer we go, the more it is Will harm us, I don't care how many days you know her, how many days have you lived together and how much do you care for the book and I don't care how much you protect her from others because everything seems to be going on When there is a wrong misunderstanding between you. I have to do it because (Love is bitter than truth) Why try hard to make life perfect, I haven't seen a better thing in my whole life....From ice cream shop to locality love was our public, I only said that No love is love, it seems to me that the feet should not be necessary for everyone, and what can I say anyway? The airings in the ears and the strange perfect glow on the face undefined is look like gorgeous, it was discovered that all makeup was a lotus. Even a single flower is a lotus thing, today everything gonna change but by the way of kindness but only identity doesn't know who is what) Still it was beautiful love ,maybe due to our mind and heart was not in control on that time and then what can be seen straight out of the leaf...and noticed with an angry gross that she was fighting with the ice cream guy because I was flirting, the reason why the shopkeeper gave me its flavor given. If the shopkeeper's brother had seen this cream, then I would not have looked towards his face and I would never have met him and nothing would have happened. Yes, I can't even do anything..... Well it is rightly said that the destiny of life is good before we are born, so what else should anyone do in this..... and I understand one thing till today not who fights for ice cream why they had whee last flavor but my fault too instead of ice cream the time was melting in his bottles undefined i don't even know what was the desire to help at that time i said that you replace me with me Abhi is not juthi ki hai. (I came to know later that it was necessary to do this, why did film made superheros , in his eyes, even today she remembers the conversation, (when I see titanic first time my eyes filll with tears ,and I dont how to contol my tears in front of someone). ..then what was she also saying that you replace your icecream only and then after a while second she said thanks to me , i think that that It was felt awkaward sometime why I dont know ?..... The biggest problem is that we girls, what should we say to us, where and they are sitting in the Mumtaz society and I am a little different, after all, I am also a human being, so I am also a boy, at that time it was felt that I am Shah Jahan and that My Mumtaz is...firstly I never thought of making Tajmahal in memory of her, I don't even remember to remember it now.

""If the time is right, I would not have loved you
(2)
And the friends who are arranging for my
death
His shadow is for you too today my slave is also
alive,

In your thoughts there will definitely be some
thing or the other.....
And if the path was the only wish
would not have said his efforts,
I would have had a lot of tears in my eyes.
yes i know i am not of existence
For the means of helplessness,
you ask for your feet once to get to me ....
I ask myself for the way" "

III

Reveal Of My Love

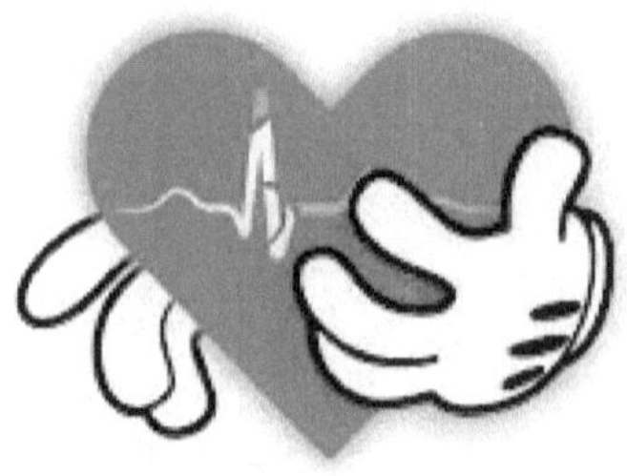

My mumtaz's name was saira it means i don't know and don't say to know saira used to belong from a family where daughters form Laxmi's form is accept and I belong from a family where people are useless donkeys and unworkable which was considered as a human being and it was not his fault either because I have never done anything for him in my life, actually I did not do anything for myself, so it is obvious what I would have done for him. Well, the profession of father of the tour was that of a militariman and my father was a professor (man all the professions in the family will work, bash should not be the profession of imparting knowledge because it is a problem when he makes a coeruleus and we can never walk on those legs, we do not have a single pain) They have trouble because we are not able to follow their rules. I have never sucked a profession in my life because I used to suck it but later she used to suck it up (it is very simple, man does not fit in any profession) . I had a dropper at that time which was completing his 2nd year as a science student (Stream: Science :Subject:PCB)Look it's quite simple right in any movie you must have seen that . Saira used to belong with a Rajput family and I used to belong with a Chandravanshi family, even though we have good bonding in our family, my father and his father are very good friends but no one said that he would marry his daughter. And did it in the family (by the way my father is happy) Wouldn't say that his only donkey is son, his marriage should be done in Rajput family. Well, even then, there is no love, so what is the use of doing all these things. The girl is .. (Because the friend is with you, no matter how bad the time is together, it is never seen in front). Is for?? If a boy proposes to you, then you can make him feel like you can't even his feet, he just put his hand toad (brocade) in love, I had seen heartbroken feet in love, I would never see someone's bonus coat, it was never imagined. Did you know that at that time the girl whom he is going to propose, he has taken a black belt in doing it, if he had known then no one would have thought, he does not even think about the wild knuckles, he has a feeling and I can not see it being fractured. After a few days, God no one tried to look at him even after lifting his eyes undefined After all this, you changed the room with them and came to live next to us because the house next door belonged to them, didn't know this batham .(I didn't know that the house where I used to play cricket in childhood was saira house). she is more faster and smarter compare in front of eyes no one beat her in his studies work, singing and many things. and sometimes I also felt like a looser in front of her achievements (Dude One, our moms are different, if any neighbor comes next to them, then they feel that they have found some relative of ours. The one who knew lost in the mushroom fair. Still, there was a different thing in that man who could never feel at the time, had a wild gift, but was cute too, used to have beautiful legs too. I used to go away. (Maybe I should have read the concept of Gravitational Law and Precipitate Charges Attract from above, then perhaps this society knows what is between us, whatever is between us, it is because of these divas)...we We didn't meet but we knew that we both are each other's kinebors and what to do, what should happen ... No one else's feet are dreams toh dreams. There is a different happiness when a girl comes in an indirect way, the flesh does not remain, but at the same time Bash says that in some way Bash should meet him, I also wanted to tell him in the baton. Looking into his eyes, the whole day and night, the things that he had done for a walk with a young boy. I did not have the courage to think of those thoughts that I could not talk to her. Well already said what was written in the order, it will remain as a gift. .... (when used to hear that she is coming, so then used to get lost in the eyes, nothing was visible in front of her) When the walk came, what did she do to see her to Ask???Never in life have you ever sweets with your hands, you have to do this to see and share with her, in the end, and why this guest is not sitting with the saint, why should he always want something to eat and drink? So, I went to prepare tea for everyone and everyone drank it, for which I had done all this. Well he liked cough, I came to know later, there is no Laila Majnu nor anyone Heer and Ranjha bash were in love, what to talk about with him??? One day I tried hard to talk to him, for some reason or the other, I don't know how to meet him, luck has a different relationship because when

Mein used to ask him to meet him and ask him to share his surgery, then luck did not mix us at all and when I used to say no, then there was such a meeting which was not expected.. They say that the farther you go from the thing, the closer it will come to you. She lived well with me. Talk about what will happen, why are you doing this kind of mischief with Ahimre. We boys are really crazy who give their life for someone else without thinking anything. What is the matter like this... For two days, the teacher kept thinking about why he didn't look at me. I am ready for it. I did not think that she would at least talk to me with a gift What happened with everyone.....I will not talk, see for myself...... After all, I am desperate to see her angry eyes to see her to the baatio?? I don't know where the conversations comes from. And see what happened the next day.........

"The hatred that is found in love belongs to the lotus, because at this time we can neither go far nor near by its paths.

I have definitely met her together only by coincidence

and even when my eyes thought of doing something
new,
I still found a way in Nayat"

IV

Unknown Truth
Hidden

21st july 2005 can never forget this day you have friends in your life, so the next day you had left the house that too soon you left the house even if there was no destination at the time, you go to classes And I was going to your classes. Then I thought that yesterday I did not see , nor did I get any chance to share with her when I have time. I'm sorry not only in my life and only in my life I mean you were born with love i.e. your boyfriends. The train of my world and my love came to a halt where no passenger was present to handle me. I don't know when this vegetable is there in the heart Why do I feel like crying in spite of all of these feelings, I am not alone with me Man does hyper what happened, I am fine alone, I will not get it, no matter what, some gift will be better than that. It is not necessary to be in love with only one. never determine her words, we don't want to leave you undefine and also thought that the girl who does not talk to someone in the locality and does not like to see any boy, she loves someone. Was with whom you had to play this game. One of the girls' ratio is work. Love had a favorite from above, that too took China. I will never forget that I will never meet her again, nor will I ever look at her Bash now thought a lot about her I stop thinking about her from yesterday, stop hurting myself by remembering my friends, if it is happy with others, then I can be happy and there is no point in crying. Emotion revealed to her , why not sanat, don't leave everything, return to his friends, don't be afraid of his friends. I could think again. And only a few days have happened. Didn't happen.) You all must also be thinking that who is so crazy for a girl. It is never normal as we understand it because if it was heat: never think about it. Nor would we ever try to make it perfect His life is always the same ... Absolutely deserted and nothing else. After thinking of all the things I thought that now what was the nahimilunaga.............phir from him that happens to everyone I am also doing the same thing and I was doing all the things during my time... Do you know what???? Trying not to see her ..just trying to try anything else not................

""Someone has said that boys are not rotten
because we have tears in our eyes,
we do not know how to say,
and where the process of Save girl Child
Taught girl Child is going on
Think about it, why are there pain?
I have accepted my love, then why are you giving
me a means of helplessness,
If there is no pond, then why are you wanting
me to be free?
I believe that I wish to attain myself
When the feet are my love,
then what is the desire to get you?""

V
Regret Of My Thinking

In love there is always one sided of truth, this thing is true, it was not known at the time, they say that the truth seen with eyes is not always true because there are many secrets behind it too. To be in love with someone is also like a mystery. Because the more we try to solve it, the more our life becomes infatuated with some kind of undefined because of the visible evidence, I was surrounded by hatred, maybe he never deserved it, the hatred with which I used to see him I was probably not there. Many times, in a hurry, we give air to such a spark, in the flames of which some of our remaining humanity gets trapped in it. On this day, seeing all that, it had become very difficult by itself, it was right before the first day that after seeing all that, whatever was left, had lost all of them in front of their eyes. To hate him, I see him every day. She used to travel to any extent to get her. Now the eyes were bringing you closer to her every time some new desires to loose her. Those too survived. I wish the day went on for a little longer, she is never far from the truth, who had intended for me to leave. It was all a sham. Holding hands, treating her in front of the camera in such a way that she doesn't care if I am there. If we keep our family constant, then we can never find out its loneliness. Even when hate happens differently, it does not take the name of being separated from someone. Squared himself used to say to go to such a place where the foot itself was not even there. I was regressed. After all, what was the reason why he never told me even after loving me so much. In the world we can trust every infidelity hyper When someone's love gets first pain, after that we never have faith in happiness. And what kind of love am I talking about, because if there was only love, then even after doing all this, I would try to know at least one reason. After all, why did she do it, why is she taking her eyes off me. When she was in love, why was she was not happy in her happiness, why did she hate her. There is a different silence, behind which there are many secrets too. It was probably wrong because everywhere I had lost my love, I never knew her feet. How much I love her. It is never in our favor. True love is never achieved. And even if it happens by mistake, then after that it is the force of the society, they just separate them. Feet our case is nothing like that, why he never revealed that, I ever revealed that I was in love with him. This was the destination of which there was no whereabouts. On the very next day of sun rises and she left after leaving without asking anything to anyone . And with the help of such lonely silence and hatred, only a regret for me going ahead (Regret) and nothing would have been proved....I wish every day would have stopped and told your feelings and maybe she would have agreed and said not to try, which I did in my whole life, even on every day I did only that.

"

"I was not able to meet you because there was a
reason behind this too,
I did not tell you my wish because I was afraid
that I might go somewhere,
I would know this thing.
It was not my life that you would go away by
making me a means of helplessness,
I had tried to hate God (2)
Feet he wished for love........
I am concerned about my own path
because I haven't found any other way to be
away from my own price............"

VI
The Way Of Love

I had cried a lot after parting with her for a few days.
Every morning whenever I opened my eyes, Bash would see
her own face, and whenever I did anything, I would feel
that I am doing the same with her. I could do anything to

get it, even I was ready to ask for my own loss, and after all, when she did not listen to me, I attempted suicide three times after that, still God's time was this wish. No one gave me death. Everyone in this world comes for one reason or the other, says all this and this thing really struck me when I came to know about its reality undefined I did all this till many days , crying in her yards, cutting hands, mining, eating only bad To keep a pond of habits, to fight or not listen to anyone, did all this. And I feel that the world would love every one whose age is not only to understand the deceit of love. The father gave her everything seemed dull, that too in front of a girl who didn't even care about us. I have a cup and praise someone else. I am not saying that every girl in the society is wrong. Absolutely not because where there is a woman like mother Sita, she is also a woman. I am not saying that only she is wrong, we are also wrong Because what we live before their arrival, we do not live after. If a person loses his humanity, then how will we call him a human and when someone gives his soul to someone else, then how will the body be after separation from him. Almost I apologized to her for two months, she did not forgive me, I go to her locality every day to see her, she never comes out. After all, what should he do if he comes to me again. I didn't know. Or was it that she would never come back to me and always used to ask God to keep a sigh of relief that wherever she is flowing, she should be happy with whom ever she is and nothing else. Feet for this, I have no complaint with this person from life, because someone else had the blessings that I needed, the destination of which my pond was his, was deserted even today. Didn't happen because love becomes distant from anyone only after getting the path of such a pond , so how it is possibe that saira is far from me on that time . Work from work, I should also get a path to work, not because of what kind of gullibe did to love someone. After passing some time It was only found out that she used to love someone else, that is, the thing that she had done right for the rest of her life, in the end, it turned out to be true.) was kept undefined and somewhere the story of my death is also related to this. Many characters had remaining story, whose glimpse you all did not even see, be patient for the future. It's because even if he had called you to pass me, he probably wouldn't go because the worst thing about her was her only. Our mentality gets so bad that even for a couple of moments of love that we can ask harm to someone to keep us happy. I used to ask myself a question at the time that how can someone be like this because the gardener has made everyone equal, then why is it like this. There are two side effects, one is positive and the other is negative, in my case their ratio is neutral ,Means she was giving me trouble and sometimes even love. could live inside it. If we get the pain mentally, then we can not handle it till our death, because until we get rid of its root, that pain will not be far from us. The damage was happening to me in the condition. At one time, it seemed that I should leave the place where his friends are our friends, that is every moment that we have spent together, we have lived together, say no matter what the condition of the time, nothing like this happened .Because the pain that I was inside could not be cured even after leaving it somewhere. I used to forget somehow. That's why I thought at the time that I should try one more time, so I thought that I will not be there now and after a few days my dad was also transferred to other city , because of which I and her too Found a reason to hear that I am going away from her now. I didn't know why I am in the conversation, see for yourself all of you......

""Waist are you, you are not worried about the nature of the feet,
you are not the protection of my way,
and the head you are talking about (2) You do not say that
That in your love is the desire of the path to God (2)
Now tell me what to do with more grace than this
because just by chance I have fallen in love with youIf you do not have feet,
then what should I complain about.""

VII
The Bitter Words

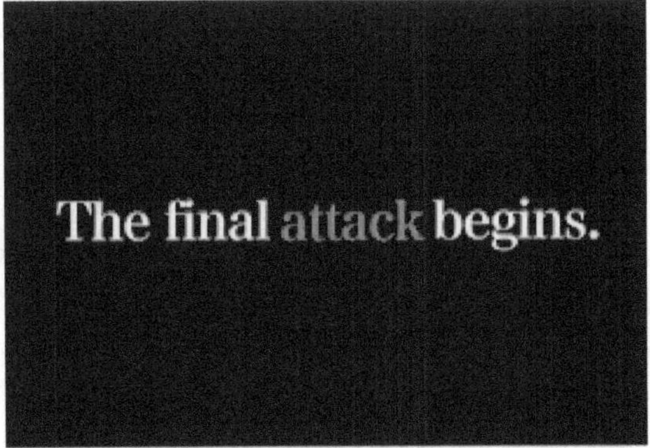

I am still not worthy of you at this time, it was not a deceit to love because I can deceive the whole world, I never believe in you, this world has never made me understand the wrong understanding from everywhere, how can you talk about your silence I'm not used to you, I can never live without you, even if you got a way for a pen, then he would have taken it in someone In the past, I tell you to forget about everything, man, if possible, forgive me for everything that I have done to you. Forgive me for all the pain that I have given you, I have been wrong and I am still there somewhere. Now I can't live without you, it's not possible when I feel alone, then I have your memory and love, then the helplessness of meeting you is more painful, I will not say anything more than this, if possible, I am sorry. Even for those who have committed mistakes, there is no apology for them. Maybe I think the reason will be right If possible, then come to meet the bash once, because the new journey is nothing more then the feet, the last bartary, only if you get it, then understand that if I do, then I will stay in your place. .... your sanat (sumo) Shocked not why this letter is like this and who is passing between us because just now we have met, what did I already know about the walk and if the public would walk Whatever happened, I got separated from him.

I will answer all this, I will see some other things behind him. I have missed a batball that in my life there were three villains and a hero was not my own journey, why girls can't be a hero, can undefined love, why did I not really love me, why did I leave my feet, he never left my side. She knew one thing very well that if she told me about you, I would never be separated from her, so she would never reveal your pain in front of me. Didn't know that . Some situations become such in life that we do not even like to see, when the same condition comes in front of a pain, then it would have been even more difficult to live life. she separated me from myself. I did a lot to do many ways, yet I never left his side. The day was completely broken, the day I saw her going to some other part, I have lost a lot in my life, love of friendship, family, teach yourself and a lot that I don't even say to reveal the thing.

When my feet lost my last hope, I had forgotten what love would have been. she took care of me all the time. Used to say that she should love someone else and maybe even a little possessive for her and some more overprotective way. And with the help of this he had thought of marrying me.

Learn one thing in life if you love someone so much without which you If you can't stay, then never reveal it to me, let it be a mystery I made a mistake due to which I saw a way to part ways undefined Talking to her, after that I spent a lot of time trying to call him every time the same status. And asked her a question which I should never ask. she had already thought I was mad at the feet of separating from me, which was the mercury behind her even at that time. You are completely right, you never say to be away from the witness with whom you are in love, not because it is your love because it is not only because the real reason is, if that one girl in the world with whom you are infatuated with her, she should also be in love with you. You say more, you give her the highest priority, not only this, even after giving your time, happiness, love, it goes away and with such an answer, the question of which we do not know. . By the way, science is right about love, it's just a game, it's just a game of hormones and nothing else. Before listening to my conversation it would seem that she must be very much in love with me, so she left me for my good The love of the one who doesn't get the reasons and troubles mein.............love is kinde a mystery Yes, it was already said and there are many reasons for this, so how can my love be a little different... she had got the reason when I asked her that you do not love anyone else other than me???(It's a matter of days when I called her and his call was busy) then the biggest mistake was mine that I asked her those questions, then what was it after that they stopped picking up my call and even blocked me and called him At the time, I used to feel that I had made a mistake. I prayed to her a lot and also apologized that I would never ask such a question in my forgiving cards.It was not For the first time on this day it seemed that I had lost my life to a deserter. Nothing could be seen except his friends and only in front of his eyes and his face was visible. I don't even know this. It was in love that the pond only takes the path of the road hai....................

""I was aware of his deceit,
but still there was a pond to get it (2)
And the way Tabassum had his grace,
that was the way of my birth.
There is a place whose politics guides everyone
and on the other side there is a path that no
one can respect."

VIII

The Memory Of
Death

Even after knowing everything about her, she never said that she should know how much she is wrong and I never even revealed to her that her presence is hurting now because what is the love in which you have not hidden the mistakes of your friends. I didn't know for how long. Says it all the time, why not be wrong After leaving the call, he was in the past (busy) for almost three months and nothing changed, after those three months, she probably forgot everything. There were also because of which I did not say that I should pay attention to someone else at the time, then I started taking care of myself. Lab, whatever happened to me in my past, I pushed myself to get out of all of them There was such a battle that I had started on my own, so why would I take help of this one.

"It was the grace of some past moments,
because of which I stayed on the road......."

When some past moments become the harifs of your future, the happiness that is about to come becomes just a wish, the whole story starts again, after almost so many months, the convey has passed away, now the convoy of my death becomes a legend. Then he had come in front of me. .This was my second such life which was still imprisoned in his memories and I did not even know about it. I don't understand anything about him. I want to express that after a few months of meeting, his deception took the place of my death..Now what happened after that day I didn't talk to him when he The day was talking to someone else, and did she read the letter I gave her and whether she had come to meet me or not, and who were those three villains in my life, and Why am I saying that his deception took my life, was it really the reason why I had died, was there any other reason, and how do I know that my death is going to happen in a few months, even then this story goes ahead This foot will grow, its tradition will end. I will not live in the world.

"Identity have been forgotten in the glory of the
plank............
Maybe even today in the matter of the love of
myself.
I am still today..
Even if you are multiplied,

I am still in the Love ""